W9-AXH-789

★ ★

★

READ ALL THE BOOKS

In The

New MATT CHRISTOPHER Sports Library!

★ ★

The New
MATT CHRISTOPHER
Sports Library

BASEBALL FLYHAWK

Illustrated by Marcy Ramsey

NORWOOD HOUSE PRESS

CHICAGO, ILLINOIS

Norwood House Press

P.O. Box 316598
Chicago, Illinois 60631

For information regarding Norwood House Press, please visit our website
at: www.norwoodhousepress.com or call 866-565-2900.

This library edition was published in 2010.

Library of Congress Cataloging-in-Publication Data:
Christopher, Matt.
  Baseball flyhawk / by Matt Christopher.
    p. cm. — (The new Matt Christopher sports library)
  ISBN-13: 978-1-59953-354-4 (library edition : alk. paper)
  ISBN-10: 1-59953-354-5 (library edition : alk. paper)
  (1. Baseball—Fiction.) I. Title.
  PZ7.C458Bar 2010
  (Fic)—dc22
                                    2009038664

Manufactured in the United States of America in North Mankato, Minnesota.
N145—010510

To

Tony and Mid

★ ★

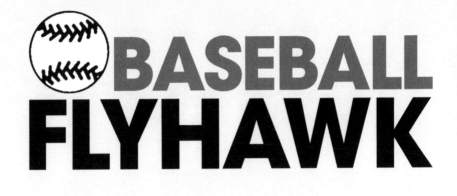

1

The score was tied, 4–4, as the Royals came to bat in the top of the fourth inning.

"Buddy! Chico! Dale!" Coach Pete Day named off the first three batters. "Come on! Let's get a man on! Let's break this tie!"

Buddy Temple picked up a yellow bat and walked to the plate. Chico Romez selected his favorite brown one, put on a helmet, and knelt in the on-deck circle. Sweat shone on his face. It was a hot day for the opening game.

But it wasn't the heat that bothered Chico. He could take the heat. He had been born in Puerto Rico and had lived there eight years before moving to the United States. And it was always hot in Puerto Rico.

No, it was the way he played baseball that bothered him.

The best way to make people like you, he figured, was to do something that would please them. Chico thought that by playing good baseball he would make a lot of friends. But so far in this game, he had done nothing to please anybody. Not even himself.

Buddy took a called strike. Then he blasted a single through the pitcher's box.

The Royals fans cheered and whistled.

"Okay, Chico," said Coach Day as he rubbed the front of his shirt.

Chico recognized the bunt signal.

Chico stood at the plate, the bat held over his shoulder. He was short and not too husky. But he was fast. If he laid one down, he might make it to first.

The Braves' pitcher toed the rubber and hurled in the ball. It was low, slightly inside. Chico put out his bat.

Tick! The ball fouled to the backstop screen.

The next pitch was high. Again Chico tried to bunt.

"Foul! Strike two!"

"Hit away, Chico!" said the coach.

Chico rubbed his toes in the dirt and held his hands close to the knob of the bat. He had failed to bunt. Now he just had to hit.

The tall Braves pitcher stepped on the rubber, looked at Buddy on first, then delivered.

The pitch was high. Chico let it go by.

"Ball!"

The next one was in there. Chico swung. A drive over short! Chico dropped his bat and sped to first. Buddy crossed second base and headed for third.

Chico touched first, then continued on toward second. The ball was bouncing out to left field. He was sure he could make it. His legs were a blur as he ran.

"Chico!" yelled the first-base coach. "Get back!"

But Chico thought that he had gone too far to turn back now.

The left fielder picked up the ball and pegged it to second. The throw was straight as a string. The second baseman caught it, put it down quickly in front of the bag, and Chico slid into it.

"Out!" snapped the base umpire.

Chico shook his head, then rose and trotted to the dugout, slapping the dust off his pants.

"One base was enough on that hit, Chico," said Coach Day. "Shouldn't have tried to stretch it."

"I'm sorry," murmured Chico.

"'Sorry'!" echoed somebody on the bench. "A lot of good that'll do."

That was String Becker. Everybody called him String because he was tall and thin. He was the Royals' first baseman, the most popular player on the team.

Chico blushed and sat down at the end of the dugout. Making a stupid out like that sure wasn't going to win him any friends.

2

Chico looked at Buddy on third. Well, if he had bunted, he might have got out anyway. And Buddy would now be on second instead of third.

Catcher Dale Hunt stepped to the plate. He popped to third for the second out.

Frankie Darsi, the Royals' southpaw pitcher and one of the best in the Grasshopper League, came up and drew a walk. Now the head of the batting order was up again, shortstop Ray Ward. Ray was small. He couldn't hit very well. But his first time up, he had drawn a walk. The second time up, he'd struck out. This time everybody hoped he would walk again.

The Braves' pitcher threw in two perfect pitches, putting little Ray on the spot. He hit the next one directly at the pitcher, who threw easily to first for the third out.

"Tough luck, Ray," said Coach Day.

The sad look on Ray's face, though, showed that the words gave him little comfort.

"Hurry in! Hurry out!" snapped the plate umpire.

Frankie walked the first man to face him. String Becker yelled to the infielders to make some noise, and they all began chattering at once.

A strikeout and two pop-ups ended the Braves' chance to score.

Center fielder Joe Ellis led off the top half

of the fifth. He grounded out to short. Then Dutch Pierce smacked one out to deep center for a triple, and the fans came to life.

This was the Royals' chance to break the tie. String Becker was up.

String threw left and batted left. So far he had blasted a double. His second time up, he had hit a high one to right field that was caught. It was no wonder now that the fielders shifted to the right and stepped farther back.

String took the first pitch. A ball.

He swung at the next one. *Crack!* The ball sailed high and deep . . . deep . . . deep! The right fielder went back . . . back. . . .

Over the fence went the ball for a home run!

"Hooray! Thataway, String! Nice blast!"

The fans stomped their feet on the stands. String crossed home plate, a smile on his face from ear to ear. Every member of the team was waiting to shake his hand.

The Royals now led, 6 to 4.

Right fielder Billy Hubble walked. Buddy and Chico grounded out to end their at-bat.

"Let's hold them!" Coach Day yelled to his boys.

Frankie worked hard on the mound. He looked tired. The sweat rolled from his face. He kept wiping it with the sleeve of his baseball jersey.

One . . . two . . . three outs. The Braves hit each time, but into someone's glove.

The sixth and last inning. Dale Hunt singled. Frankie lined one to short. The ball was scarcely six feet off the ground. The shortstop caught it, pegged it to first, and Dale was out.

Double play!

Coach Day had Kenny Morton pinch-hit

for Ray. Kenny singled through short. Then Joe Ellis struck out.

"All right, boys! This is it!" said Coach Day. "Plug up all the holes!"

"Let's hear the chatter!" cried String.

The Braves' lead-off man struck at the first pitch. *Crack!* A high foul ball right over Dale's head.

He waited for it to come down. Caught it! One out.

Then Frankie got a little careless, maybe because he was tired. He walked the next man. The next pounded out a single, a Texas leaguer over second. String called time and walked to the mound. He said something to Frankie, then returned to his position at first.

The Braves fans were yelling excitedly, trying hard to offer encouragement to their players.

Chico, in left field, felt his heart pounding

hard. With two men on, the Braves could tie the score and go on to win.

"Strike him out, Frankie!" he yelled. "Strike him out!"

A left-hand hitter stepped to the plate. The fielders moved slightly to the right. Frankie pitched.

The batter swung. Bat met ball, and Chico saw the little white pill soar high into the air. It sailed toward left field about halfway between Chico and the infield!

Chico ran in hard. "I got it!" he yelled. "I got it!"

For a moment he wasn't sure he would get it. He ran harder. Then he put out his glove, and the ball dropped into it.

"Great catch, Chico!" yelled Dutch Pierce from third.

"Thataboy, Chico!" He heard String all the way from first.

Chico's heart tingled.

He ran back to his position. *It's a good thing I caught that ball,* he thought.

He felt so good about it, he didn't realize which batter had come to the plate. The Braves' number one slugger. A right-hand hitter.

Frankie breezed in a pitch, and the tall Braves hitter smacked it. The ball left the bat as if it were shot from a gun. Chico could tell instantly that it was going over his head.

He turned around and started running as fast as he could. It wasn't fast enough. The ball dropped and bounced on. By the time he picked it up and pegged it in, he was too late.

It was a home run. It won the game for the Braves, 7 to 6.

Chico trotted in from the outfield. He heard someone shout his name, then say things that sank deeply inside him and hurt.

"Where were you playing for that man?

Behind shortstop?" It was String Becker. His face was red with rage.

"I was playing my right position," murmured Chico.

"Right position, my eye!" shouted String. "You weren't playing deep at all. If you were playing where you should've been, you would've caught that ball easy."

Chico stared at the others around him. One by one they turned and looked away.

Chico could see they all felt as String did. They blamed him for losing the game.

Chico," said Coach Day, "help me put this equipment away, will you?"

"Okay, Coach."

They put the catcher's equipment, the bats, and the balls into the large canvas bag.

"Don't take to heart what String and the other boys say," advised the coach. "They don't really mean it."

Chico frowned and stayed silent.

"They just forget themselves for a minute," said the coach. "They get kind of excited. I'll talk to them about it."

"No, Coach. Please. Don't say anything to them."

"Why not?"

Chico shrugged. The sun shone brightly in his eyes, making him squint. "I don't want them to think I spoke to you about it. They — they wouldn't like that."

Coach Day smiled. "Okay. If you say so. Want a ride home?"

"No, thanks," said Chico. "I just live two blocks away."

The coach got into his station wagon and drove off. Chico walked, his glove swinging from his wrist.

He got to thinking about the way String had yelled at him and the way the other boys had looked at him. *Every little mistake I make, they make it sound much worse.*

He was walking by Jim's Ice Cream Shop when a voice from inside yelled to him.

"Hey, Chico! Come in. Have a sundae."

Chico looked through the screen door and saw six or seven members of the Royals sitting at the bar, enjoying sundaes. It was Buddy Temple who had called to him.

Chico glanced over the faces. He saw String Becker, and that was enough.

"No, thanks!" he said, and started walking faster.

A moment later Buddy was out on the sidewalk, yelling to him. "Chico! Hey, Chico!"

But Chico walked on, not looking back once.

He reached home, went to the back porch, and sat down. His heart pounded as if he'd been running. His forehead was covered with sweat. He wiped it with his arm.

Then he looked at the glove in his hand and sucked in his breath.

This wasn't his glove!

He rose to his feet, trembling. Whose glove was it? And what had happened to his?

A lump rose in Chico's throat. What an opening day this was for him! He had been blamed for the loss of the Royals' first game. Now he had come home with somebody else's glove.

The door behind him opened on squeaking hinges. He turned around. His mother smiled at him.

"Chico! When did you get home?"

"A little while ago," said Chico. He turned and sat down again, his lower lip quivering.

She came and sat beside him. "Chico, is something wrong?"

He told her about the game, and the glove. Her dark-brown eyes looked at him sadly. She put an arm around his shoulder and pressed him to her.

"Don't worry," his mother said. "You'll

figure out who owns the glove, and you'll find yours. It was only a mistake." She stood up. "Come inside, Chico. You must be hungry."

Chico washed, changed into other clothes, then sat at the table in the dining room. On the wall behind him was a large white cloth on which were embroidered the Spanish words DIOS BENDIGA NUESTRO HOGAR. And underneath it, in English, GOD BLESS OUR HOME.

Chico's father came in from the living room. His hair was black and wavy. His eyes, behind wire-rimmed glasses, were brown and smiling.

"You look sad, Chico," Mr. Romez said. "You lost the ball game?"

"Yes," said Chico. "A home run over my head in the last inning beat us."

"That's too bad," said his father. "Well — better luck next time."

While he ate the meat and beans and the

tossed salad, Chico worried about his glove. Had somebody else picked it up? Was it the person who owned the glove he had picked up?

Chico couldn't swallow his food for a minute. Why was he always doing something wrong?

Then he thought about his teammates. Especially String. Chico was sure String didn't like him at all.

But he remembered something, and with pride he thought: *At least I can do one thing well. Diving! And I have two trophies to prove it!*

There was a knock on the door. Mrs. Romez went to answer it.

"Chico," she called, "someone to see you!"

Chico stared. The trembling returned.

4

The boy at the door was Buddy Temple.

"Hi, Chico. How about coming over later? We can play catch, and I'll show you my electric train set."

Chico's face lit up. He turned around to his mother and father. "May I?"

His mother smiled. She looked at her husband. He smiled, too, and nodded.

"Good!" said Buddy. "I'll see you later, then." He started to leave.

"Buddy," said Chico, "wait!"

Chico went to the kitchen and returned with the glove he had picked up by mistake.

"I brought this glove home," said Chico. "But it's not mine. Do you know whose it is?"

"Well, I know it's not mine," replied Buddy. He took it and examined it thoroughly. "No name on it. No, I don't know whose it is, Chico. Keep it until the next game. Somebody should claim it then."

"Okay," said Chico. "But somebody has mine, too. Did you see one of the guys with a different glove? Did anybody say anything?"

Buddy shook his head. "No — but don't worry. You'll get your glove back. And you'll find the owner of that one, too. See you later, Chico!"

Chico watched Buddy hop off the porch and head for home. A smile touched his lips. All at once he wasn't lonely anymore. He liked Buddy Temple. And he knew Buddy liked him.

He went to Buddy's house later. They played pitch-and-catch. Then Buddy took Chico into the basement and showed him his electric train set. It was on a large platform, the size of a Ping-Pong table, which stood about two feet off the floor. The trains were all kinds: passenger, freight, cattle cars. Buddy turned on a switch on one of the two transformers, and the passenger train began to move along the track. He turned on a switch on the second transformer, and the freight train began to move. The trains crossed bridges, went through tunnels, and passed by tiny buildings.

Whoo-o! Whoo-o! their whistles shrilled.

Chico watched with fascination as the freight train stopped and a cargo of cattle moved off a loading platform onto a car.

"Maybe someday my father will buy me a set like this," said Chico hopefully.

Buddy smiled. "My dad started this for me a long time ago," he said. "Every Christmas he gets me something new. It's lots of fun. Especially in the winter."

"I've got to go home," said Chico. "Can I come again? I never saw a train set like this before."

"You'd better come again, Chico." Buddy's eyes were warm and friendly. "Any time."

The next day, Chico thought about his glove and the one that didn't belong to him. *I hope it's not String's. And I hope he doesn't have mine.*

Then he realized that it couldn't be String's glove, because String's was a first-base mitt.

Chico went to the swimming pool at the park in the afternoon. His mother went with him. There were two diving boards: one low, the other high. Chico climbed up the high one. He stood on the tip of the board, the sun warm against his body.

He stretched his hands straight out in front of him, looked down at the water, and saw his reflection in it. A smile cracked his lips, then he gave himself a spring and dived off the board.

He struck the water like a whisper, went to the bottom, and came up, blowing air out of his lungs.

"Nice going, kid!" the lifeguard said, smiling. Chico smiled back.

He stayed there a long time, diving and swimming. He forgot about String and about his glove. Being in the water took his mind off all his worries.

But a few days later, his anxiety returned. It was the day of the second game.

When Chico arrived at the field, he saw

most of the Royals players at the first-base side, warming up. The Colts were behind third. Chico looked around anxiously. Everybody had a glove and was playing catch.

"Let's hit!" Coach Day yelled. "Fielders, get out there! Buddy, lay one down and hit two! Kenny, throw 'em in!"

The fielders scrambled to the field. Kenny Morton walked to the mound and began pitching them in.

Chico stood there a moment, holding the glove that didn't belong to him. Then he started trotting out to the outfield.

"Hey, Chico!" a voice suddenly yelled behind him. "Come here!"

Chico stopped in his tracks and whirled around. Dutch Pierce was walking toward him. He had just come onto the field. He was looking with dark, piercing eyes at the glove on Chico's hand.

"That looks like my glove," Dutch

snapped. He whipped it off Chico's hand. "It is!" His eyes blazed as he looked at Chico. "Where did you get it? How long have you had it?"

Chico stepped back. Dutch was four inches taller than he.

"I — I picked it up by mistake after our first game," he stammered.

"By mistake?" Dutch's lips tightened. Without another word, he ran out to the field.

For a moment Chico stood there trembling.

Where is my glove? he thought, and began to worry more than ever.

Chico."

Chico turned, and squinted against the sun at Coach Day.

"There's a glove in the equipment bag," said the coach. "It's probably yours."

Chico ran to the bag, opened it, and pulled out a glove. It was his!

"Thanks, Coach," he murmured. "I — I was afraid I wouldn't find it."

Coach Day grinned. "I found it lying on the ground by the bench. If I'd known it was yours, I would have taken it to you. Okay, get your hits now, then shag a few."

After the Royals had their hitting practice, the Colts took the field. A little while later, the game started.

The sky was clear blue and the sun a bright, blazing ball of orange. A perfect day for baseball.

The Royals had first raps. On the mound for the Colts was Teddy Nash, a tall, freckle-faced southpaw. His warmup pitches breezed in like white bullets.

Lead-off man Ray Ward strode to the plate. Teddy Nash made short work of him. Joe and Dutch didn't get to first base, either. It looked as if Teddy was going to have a good day.

Out in the field, Chico realized that he and the other fielders might have some trouble. They had to face the bright sun.

Don Drake, a right-hander, pitched for the Royals. He walked the first man and then the second. The third man hit into a double play. Then a single scored a run. Catcher Dale Hunt caught a foul pop fly, and the first inning was over.

String Becker was first man up for the Royals. He swung two bats from one shoulder to the other as he walked toward the plate. He tossed one back and stepped into the box. He tapped the plate with the big end of his bat, then waited for Teddy Nash to pitch.

Teddy blazed two over the plate. String swung at both and missed. Then Teddy wasted a couple, making the count two and two.

"Come on, String! Make it be in there!" said the coach.

The next pitch *was* in there. String belted it, a hot grounder down to first. The first baseman reached for it. The ball touched his mitt, but then it buzzed past. String dashed to first.

"Okay, men, there's our starter," said the coach. "Let's keep it up."

Billy Hubble tried. So did Buddy and Chico. But Teddy's arm was working for him. None of the three hit, and String died on first.

The game continued swiftly. Both pitchers were hot. Teddy had no curve to speak of. But he had a side-arm delivery that made it seem as if the ball were coming from near first base. Most of the Royals players were shy of the ball, thinking it would hit them. But Teddy's control was fine, and the pitches were strikes most of the time.

Don's delivery was overhand. He had learned to throw two curves. One was a screwball, a pitch that curved in toward a right-hand batter. The other curved away. That one was better, because it had a drop to it, too.

In the fourth inning, things began to pop.

Teddy got a three-two count on Dutch, then threw an inside pitch: a free ticket to first.

String came up. So far only he had got a hit off Teddy Nash. Teddy blazed in two pitches, both balls. Then String took a called strike. The next pitch was in there, too, and String powdered it. The ball sizzled just inside the first-base line for a clean single. Dutch went around to third; String held up at first.

"Okay, boys," said Coach Day. "Two ducks on, and none away. Let's bring them in."

Billy Hubble tagged the first pitch. It was a pop fly in the infield, an automatic out.

The boys in the dugout groaned.

Buddy waited till a strike was called on him, then socked a chest-high pitch down to short. A perfect throw to first put him out.

"Come on, somebody!" yelled String disgustedly. "Can't anybody hit that ball?"

It was Chico's turn to bat. He started for the plate.

"Chico! Wait!"

Chico turned. His jaw sagged. He looked pleadingly at the coach. *Don't let somebody pinch-hit for me,* he thought. *I am sure I can hit that ball now.*

Chico started back toward the dugout.

"No, never mind," said the coach, waving Chico back to the plate. "Get up there, Chico. Show 'em you can do it."

A sudden happy gleam came to Chico's eyes. He turned, went to the plate, and dug his toes into the dirt.

"Strike one!"

Chico thought that the pitch had been a little inside, but he adjusted his stance and concentrated on the next pitch.

Then — there it was — coming in belt-high, crossing the plate almost down the middle. Chico swung. *Crack!* A long, high blast going over the left fielder's head!

Chico dropped his bat and ran. One run

came in! Another! Chico crossed first, second, and went to third. The third-base coach waved him on to home. Chico kept going, his black hair flying wildly. Somewhere on the base paths he had lost his helmet and cap.

"Stay up, Chico! Stay up!" cried the guys crowding around home plate, waiting to shake his hand.

A home run!

"What a smack, Chico!" String said. "Nice —"

Suddenly there was silence. One of the Colts infielders was signaling to the crowd around the plate.

"What's he saying?" Coach Day asked.

"He's out!" cried the umpire at first.

"Who's out?" said Coach Day. No one else spoke. Even the bleachers were silent as the fans watched, wondering what had happened.

"That kid who just hit that home run," said the umpire, running in and pointing at Chico Romez. "The first baseman saw it, and I saw it. He never touched first base!"

Chico stared. His heart sank to his shoes.

"What a crazy, stupid thing!" yelled Dutch. "A home run — and he didn't touch first base!"

6

The score was still one to nothing in the Colts' favor.

Chico's heart was crushed. He wished that Coach Day would remove him from the game. He was so ashamed of the foolish mistake he had made, he didn't care if the coach benched him for the next two or three games.

But the coach left him in.

"Watch it the next time, Chico," advised Coach Day. "Touch every base."

"Yes, sir," murmured Chico. But it was

like locking the barn after the horse had already run away.

The Colts got a man on. Their long-ball hitter was up, and Chico stepped back deeper into left. *Crack!* The white pill shot toward left center field as if from a cannon. Chico and center fielder Joe Ellis raced after it.

Somebody from the infield yelled, "Let Chico take it! Let Chico take it!"

Chico reached out his glove, caught the ball, and just missed colliding with Joe. He pegged the ball in.

"Beautiful catch, Chico!" The fans applauded him.

Then a ground ball went for a single, and the Colts scored a run. Two to nothing, Colts' favor.

In the top of the fifth, Dale singled. That gave the Royals a starter. They went ahead and scored. String made the last out of their turn at bat.

Don's hooks baffled the Colts' hitters. Not a man reached first. The close game kept the fans on edge.

This was the Royals' last chance.

Kenny Morton pinch-hit for Billy Hubble and whacked a double. Coach Day put in another pinch-hitter, Louie Carlo. Louie took a strike, then popped up to the pitcher. One away.

Chico strode to the plate.

"Come on, Chico! Another blast! Another homer! This time touch the bases!"

The pitch. "Ball!" said the umpire.

Another pitch. Chico powdered it — a ground ball through short. Kenny touched third and went in toward home. Chico dashed for first, the fans' cheers ringing in his ears.

Chico made sure he touched first. He headed for second, his helmet flying off his head.

"Chico!" yelled the first-base coach. "Play it safe! Watch that throw-in!"

The left fielder pegged the ball in to second. A perfect throw!

Chico, two thirds of the way to second, came to a sudden stop. *What have I done?* he thought. The second baseman ran Chico back, then tossed the ball to the first baseman. Chico was caught in a hot box.

Back and forth the first and second basemen passed the ball, trapping Chico. Then suddenly the first baseman's peg went wild! The ball hit the ground and bounced to the right of the bag. Chico raced to the keystone sack. Safe!

"Wow!" murmured Chico. He bent forward and rested his hands on his knees. *That* was sure close!

Meanwhile, Kenny had breezed into home, tying the score at 2 to 2.

Dale was up next. He popped out. Two outs. Then Don socked one over second. It was just out of reach of the second baseman, and Chico scored as the Royals fans cheered and applauded. His run pulled the Royals ahead, 3 to 2.

The team's last chance at bat came to an end when Ray Ward struck out.

"Hold them!" yelled the Royals fans. "Hold them!"

"Three men to get, Don!" yelled String. "Just three!"

Don's hook fanned the first batter. The next hitter clouted one over short, a clean hit. The batter slid in to second safely for a double.

String called time. He went to the mound and talked with Don. Then he returned to first. Time in was called.

Don stepped on the rubber and delivered. A hot one-bouncer came right back at him! Don caught it and tossed it to first. Two away.

One more to get!

A right-hander stepped to the plate. Don pitched. *Crack!* A long drive to left field. Chico started back, then turned and watched the white pill come down from the sky.

Suddenly it was lost in the blinding sun! For an instant Chico had a glimpse of it again. He put out his hand. *Whoosh!* The ball struck the glove's little finger, hit the ground, and bounced past him.

Chico ran after it, picked it up, and pegged it in. The throw was too late. The hitter was running home from third. He crossed the plate before the ball reached Dale.

The game was over. The Colts were the winners, 4 to 3.

"How did you miss it?" stormed String, his face twisted. "You should have caught it easily!"

"It was the sun," murmured Chico lamely. "I lost it in the sun."

String just shook his head and walked away in disgust.

7

Four days after the loss to the Colts, the Royals were on the field again, this time playing against the Lions. The stands were full of fans, including Mr. and Mrs. Romez and many other players' parents who weren't usually at the games. It was the Fourth of July, which meant most people had the day off from work. A brass band played in the park, adding an air of festivity as both teams warmed up before the game.

A few minutes before the game started, both teams walked out to the field. The Lions stood along the third-base line and the

Royals along the first-base line. In front of them, standing near the mound, were the coaches of both teams. They all faced center field.

Chico was about to ask Buddy what was going on when the brass band began to play "The Star-Spangled Banner." The coaches and the players took off their caps and held them against their chests. A flag was slowly raised up a pole behind the center field fence.

Chico watched it while the music filled the park. He wasn't sure of all the words to the national anthem. But there was something about the song and the flag raising that made a lump appear in his throat.

When the ceremony was over, Chico cheered with the rest of the team and ran back to the dugout. But his good mood was shattered when he caught a glaring look from String. As a matter of fact, he wasn't sure anybody on the team, except Buddy, gave him a glad-to-see-you look. He worried that they were still holding him responsible for the loss on Thursday. That he had lost the ball in the sun was no excuse.

As he was picking up his glove, he heard Dutch ask String if he was going over to the pool after the game.

"Nah," String replied. "Swimming and diving are for sissies." He glanced over at Chico and smirked.

Chico felt his face flush. He was about to turn away when Buddy piped up. "Well, I'm going. I can't imagine spending the Fourth of July anywhere else but poolside. Hey, Chico, don't forget, you promised you'd show me how to do that back dive today!"

Chico knew he had never made any such promise. But there was nothing he would have rather done today than swim with Buddy. "You bet!" Chico replied. *And thanks for sticking up for me,* he added silently.

The game started. The Royals took the field first, with the lineup the same as last time. Only today, southpaw Frankie Darsi was on the mound.

Frankie blazed the ball in overhand and had no trouble getting the Lions out that first inning.

The Royals came up and scored two runs. In the third they scored three more to put them in the lead, 5 to 0.

"We'd better take this game," muttered String in the dugout, loud enough for everybody to hear. "We can't give it away now."

Chico felt that String intended those words especially for him.

In the top of the fourth, the Lions threatened to put across some runs. Two hits in a row put men on first and third. Then

Frankie walked a man, and the bases were loaded.

The heavy hitters of the Lions were up. Frankie reared back and threw. *Crack!* The pitch was smacked to deep left. Chico went after it. He knew what it would mean if he failed to catch this fly ball.

The ball curved toward the left-field foul line, but it was still well in fair territory. Chico ran as hard as he could, put up both his hands, and caught the ball. He stopped quickly and pegged the ball in to third. Dutch caught it and tagged the runner bolting in from second.

The runner on third had scored though, after tagging up.

"Nice throw, Chico!" Dutch yelled to him.

Five to one. Then a pop-up ended the Lions' threat.

Chico singled in the bottom of the fourth. He ran partway to second before the first-base coach's cries registered in his mind. "Get back here, Chico! Get back here!"

Chico got back to first. *Almost played it foolish again,* he thought.

Dale Hunt came to bat and blasted the first pitch. The ball streaked in a clothesline drive toward short. Chico took off. As he neared the keystone sack, he heard shouting behind him. He looked out to left field, expecting to see one of the outfielders fielding the ball.

But the ball wasn't out there!

Chico looked at the smiling face of the Lions' second sacker and knew instantly that something funny had happened.

He turned and saw the Lions' first baseman standing on the bag, the ball in his hand.

Chico's eyes widened. "What happened?" he murmured.

"What happened?" The Lions' second

baseman laughed. "You're out, that's what happened! Our shortstop caught the line drive and doubled you off at first!"

Chico stared. He slapped his helmet angrily against his thigh and ran across the diamond to the dugout.

"Chico!" said Coach Day. "Why didn't you watch it? That ball was in the air!"

"I'm sorry," said Chico. There was nothing else he could say. The coach just shook his head and walked a few paces away.

"Messes up practically every time!" Chico heard String say in a low voice. "We'll probably lose this game yet."

But the Royals, including Chico, played airtight ball after that and went on to win, 5 to 2.

After the game, Chico saw his mother and father waiting for him. They gave him their permission to join Buddy at the pool. Chico and Buddy arranged to meet there after they'd gone home and changed.

"You played a good game, son," Mr. Romez said as they walked home.

Chico shrugged. "It would be better if I didn't mess up so much."

His parents laughed.

"Everyone makes mistakes," his mother commented.

Twenty minutes later, Chico and Buddy were splashing in the pool along with many of their teammates. Chico felt his worries leave him as he climbed the ladder to the diving board.

"Do a somersault, kid!" he heard the lifeguard call. Chico nodded and walked to the end of the board. He knew everybody was watching him. He took a deep breath, bounced once, then flung himself into the air and curled into a tight ball. Once, twice around! He hit the water with barely a splash.

When his head popped through the surface, he heard cheering and applause. Buddy swam toward him and playfully tried to duck him under. But Chico turned the tables and ducked him instead.

Sputtering and laughing at the same time, the boys swam to the edge to catch their breath. Buddy poked Chico in the ribs.

"Look who's here!" he said in surprise.

Chico looked where he was pointing and saw String. He was sitting at the edge of the pool, his long legs dangling in the water. His hair was still dry.

"Hey, String!" Buddy called. "I thought swimming was just for sissies!"

String looked uncomfortable, and then he shrugged. "Nothing wrong with wanting to cool off a little." He stood up. "Besides, I'm just here to see who wants to come to a cookout at my house later on. We can see the fireworks from my backyard."

Chico glanced at Buddy. Was String including him in the invitation, or was it just for Buddy?

"We'll be there, won't we, Chico?" Buddy said.

String shrugged again. "Yeah, sure, bring him along." He turned and walked away.

Chico felt his face redden. Darn that String! Why does he always make me feel like an outsider?

A call from one of his teammates interrupted his thoughts. "Hey, Chico! Bet you can't do a back dive!"

Chico smiled. At least here he felt like he belonged.

He and Buddy stayed at the pool for another half hour. Chico performed jackknife dives, both forward and backward, and then a few more somersaults. He felt happy now. He was doing something he could do well.

Perhaps someday he could do as well playing baseball.

After they left the pool, Buddy and Chico stopped first at Chico's house to get his parents' permission to go to String's barbecue, then at Buddy's. Buddy grabbed a package of marshmallows from his pantry to bring over.

"Should I get something to bring, too?" Chico asked anxiously.

"No, I'm sure there'll be plenty of food. I just like toasted marshmallows so much I'm likely to eat a bag of them by myself!"

Dutch Pierce, Frankie Darsi, Ray Ward, and Joe Ellis were already eating hot dogs and hamburgers when Buddy and Chico arrived. String directed them to where his dad was standing next to the grill. "Hurry up, or you'll miss out on all the food. Marshmallows again this year, huh, Buddy?" String glanced at Chico's empty hands but didn't say anything.

String's father filled their plates with hot dogs, hamburgers, and potato salad. "Plenty more where that came from, boys," he said cheerfully.

The sky gradually darkened, and the boys all found places to sit on the lawn. Craning their necks backward and munching on marshmallows and watermelon, they oohed and aahed at the fireworks display. Chico was spellbound at the colors and laughed with the others at the loud bangs that thundered through the sky after each display.

Later, he and Buddy walked home together.

"Hey, Chico, I was wondering if you could do me a favor," Buddy said. "Mom, Dad, and us kids are going to visit my uncle for a couple of days. Would you mind delivering my papers for two mornings? You'd get to keep all the money you earn those two days. You could come with me on the route to-morrow morning and I could show you the ropes. How about it?"

"Sure," said Chico. "I'll do it."

Chico had answered before giving it any thought. After all, Buddy was his best friend. He would help Buddy no matter what it was.

But — deliver papers? Suddenly he was worried. Would just one day of going around with Buddy be enough to help Chico re-member all the customers?

"How many customers do you have, Buddy?" asked Chico.

"Sixty-four," said Buddy.

"Sixty-four!" Chico's eyes went wide.

Buddy laughed. "Some kids have seventy or eighty! It's not too bad. They're all within a few blocks of each other. You won't have any trouble, Chico. Then you'll do it?"

Chico smiled. "Of course!"

"Thanks, Chico! Oh — you have to be up early! We pick up our papers at seven o'clock."

"I'll be up," promised Chico.

The next morning, Buddy was at the front door at ten minutes of seven. Chico was up, waiting for him. They walked two blocks to the corner of Hanley and Lincoln Streets. Four boys were there already, newspaper bags slung over their shoulders. They spoke to Buddy, but looked strangely at Chico.

"This is Chico Romez," said Buddy. "He's going to deliver my papers for me the next two mornings. I'm going to be gone for a couple of days with my family. We're leaving really early tomorrow morning — even earlier than this!"

The guys laughed and said hi to Chico. Chico felt better.

A few minutes later, a station wagon drove up. A man got out, greeted the boys, and hauled out several piles of newspapers. The papers had a peculiar smell. Buddy said it was the ink.

Buddy explained to the man why Chico was with him, then piled the newspapers into his bag. Chico watched carefully.

Then the man took several tickets out of his coat pocket and gave one to each boy. Except Chico.

"For the Jay Jam Circus tonight," he said. He looked at Chico. "Sorry. These are only for our regular carriers. We don't have any extras."

Chico shrugged. "That's all right," he said.

Chico and Buddy crossed the street. Buddy took the ticket out of his pocket. "Here, Chico," he said. "You take it."

"No," said Chico. "It's yours. Why do you want to give it to me?"

Buddy looked at him a moment, then returned the ticket to his pocket.

He got back to his business of delivering papers. He showed Chico how he folded them and tossed them onto the porches.

Chico learned by doing. He folded the papers, too, and tossed them onto the porches of Buddy's customers the way Buddy did. It was fun.

It took almost an hour to deliver all the papers. Buddy took Chico home with him and gave him a list of names and addresses.

"There you go," said Buddy. "You can't go wrong. And here's the bag. Good luck!"

Chico smiled. "Thanks. With this list I shouldn't have any trouble."

Chico took the list and the newspaper bag home with him, and put them in his room.

That afternoon the Royals played the Marlins and won, 12 to 1. Errors and foolish plays took the heart out of the Marlins. The Royals' record now was two wins, two losses.

That evening Chico met Buddy, String, Frankie, and Dale coming up the street.

"Hi, Chico!" said Frankie. "We're going to the circus. Can you come along?"

"I don't have a ticket," said Chico sadly.

"No ticket, no circus!" String said, laughing.

Chico glowered at him.

"Can you get some money from your folks, Chico?" asked Buddy. "You can pay them back out of what you'll make from selling those papers."

Chico smiled. "Maybe! Will you wait for me? I'll ask them."

"Go ahead," said Buddy. "We'll wait."

Chico ran into the house. His mother and father were both home. Breathlessly he asked them if he could go to the circus with Buddy, String, Frankie, and Dale.

His parents smiled. "You don't want to go with *us*?"

Chico's brows raised. His eyes widened. "You're going, too?"

His mother went to the cabinet in the dining room and brought out three tickets. "We were planning to leave in a little while," she said. "Would you rather go with us or your friends?"

Chico stared. What a choice to make!

"I'll go with you and Papa," he said, and started to turn away. "I'll tell the guys."

"Wait, Chico," said his father. "Mama, give him his ticket. Let him go with his friends. I think he'll enjoy it better."

Chico's eyes brightened. He took the ticket. "You sure it's all right, Papa? Mama?"

"We're sure," said his mother, nodding.

"Thank you!" he shouted, and ran out to join his friends.

The big tent of the Jay Jam Circus was

packed with fun. Elephants danced, tigers and lions leapt through hoops, acrobats performed on flying trapezes, a man and a woman pedaled bicycles on a tightwire high above the ground. Chico had seen something like this on television, but this was the first time he had ever seen it live.

That night he went to bed thinking about the amazing performances. It was a long time before he fell asleep.

When he woke up, the first thing on his mind was the circus. He chatted about it with his mother as he ate breakfast. His father had already left for work.

Suddenly he remembered something — something he had to do!

"Mama! Mama! What time is it?" he asked, jumping out of the chair.

"It's eight o'clock," she said.

"Eight o'clock?" Chico's heart leapt to his

throat. "Mama! I'm supposed to deliver Buddy's papers today. I should have been at the street corner at seven!"

"Oh, my poor boy!" his mother cried. "And look what's happening outside!"

Chico ran to the window and choked back tears.

Raindrops as big as nickels were pouring from the sky.

Chico put on his raincoat and boots. He folded the newspaper bag, tucked it under the raincoat, and ran out into the rain. Suddenly he remembered the list of names and addresses, and ran back into the house for it.

What a terrible thing to forget his promise to Buddy!

Horrible thoughts rolled around in his mind. Certainly the man who brought the papers would not be waiting for him. It was Chico's responsibility to be there at seven o'clock. One hour ago! The papers were probably soaked from the rain.

Chico's heart was never so sick.

He ran all the way to the street corner where the newspapers were supposed to be. There was no one there, of course. Not even a pile of newspapers.

Chico's eyes darted around frantically. Hadn't the man left the papers?

Then he saw them. They were against the trunk of a tree where the rain wouldn't hit them so heavily. Some old newspapers were draped over them, with a rock on top to keep them from blowing off.

Chico breathed easier. At least the man had thought about him.

Chico took out the newspaper bag, un-folded it, and piled the papers into it. When the papers were all inside, he took off his raincoat, picked up the bag, and put the strap over his shoulder. Then he put the raincoat back on and started out on his route. The papers were heavy. The strap of the bag began to hurt his shoulders.

The raincoat helped to keep the papers from getting wet, but the paper with the list of names started to get wet and soggy. Chico's thumb smudged some of the names, and he had trouble reading them.

Little by little, though, the pain in his shoulder eased up as fewer and fewer papers were left in the bag. Once the rain slacked for a few minutes, and Chico thought it would stop. Then it poured again as heavily as before. It was still pouring when Chico finished delivering the papers.

At last! Not only was his bag light; his heart was, too.

But he still had tomorrow morning's delivery to make. He hoped it wouldn't rain then.

"You're home!" his mother exclaimed as she opened the front door for him. "My poor boy! Were the papers all wet?"

Chico grinned through the rainwater that glistened on his face. "Not too bad, Mama. I had them covered very well."

It rained the rest of that day, but it was beautiful the next morning. The sun was out, and birds were singing. Chico arrived at the street corner ahead of time, picked up the newspapers, and went on his route.

He referred often to the list of names and addresses to make sure he delivered the papers to the right customers. He had written over the smudged names so they were easy to read now. This time the job was fun.

Later that afternoon, Buddy came over with a ball and glove. He wanted to know how

Chico had made out the day before, when it had rained so hard.

"You know what happened? I forgot about it," Chico said. "I woke up late. When I reached the corner, it was eight o'clock. But the man had put the papers under a tree and covered them up. I'm sorry I was late, Buddy. But I delivered the papers okay."

Buddy smiled. "I'm sorry it rained, Chico. Of all the times!"

"Thanks, but it was okay. Did you have a nice time at your uncle's?"

"Wonderful," said Buddy. "My uncle has a boat. We had picnics, and rode around most of the time. You'll have to come with me next time!"

Chico glowed with happiness. They played catch for a while, then Buddy headed home.

The Royals tackled the Bombers on Tuesday. The game started with the Bombers living up to their name. They knocked in three runs in the first inning and two more in the second. They were pounding Don Drake's pitches all over the lot.

Frankie Darsi replaced Don. His south-paw delivery stunned the Bombers for a while. They either grounded out or struck out. The Royals came through with two runs in the third and one in the fourth, bringing the score up to 5 to 3. They clinched the game in the last inning when String smashed out a home run with two men on — sending them over the top, 6 to 5.

On Friday the Royals tangled with the Braves as the second round began. There were three rounds altogether.

Don Drake started on the mound. The Royals picked up two runs in the second inning. They held the Braves to two hits until the third inning, when Dutch Pierce fumbled a grounder, which started things for the Braves. They socked out a double, scoring a run. A walk and then a wild peg to first by shortstop Ray Ward filled the bases.

The cleanup man stepped to the plate and smashed a long, powerful drive out to left field. It looked like a grand slammer!

Chico turned and put his back to the ball as he raced toward the fence. Then he looked over his shoulder, turned, and made a sparkling one-handed catch.

The runners tagged up. The man on third raced for home. Dutch caught Chico's throw-in and held the ball. It was too late to get the man scoring the run. The other runners had advanced. So now there were men on second and third.

The fans cheered Chico's catch. "Thataway, Chico! Nice catch!"

A one-hopper to Don, which he threw easily to first, and then a strikeout, ended the bad inning.

The score was tied at 2 to 2.

"Beautiful catch out there, Chico," Coach Day said as Chico trotted in. "You robbed him of a homer."

Chico smiled.

Buddy Temple led off and flied out to center. Then Chico came up. He took a strike, then smacked a grounder that just missed the pitcher's legs. A single!

Dale Hunt hit a sizzling grounder to third. The Braves' third sacker bobbled the ball. By the time he had it in his hand, it was too late to throw anywhere.

Chico stood on second, breathing hard. His right shoe felt loose. He saw that the laces had come untied.

He didn't want to call time out, though.

He would wait until he got to the dugout, then tie the laces.

Don blasted the first pitch. A high fly to center field. The center fielder made the catch. Chico tagged up and made a beeline for third. He had to beat that throw-in!

Then, halfway to the bag, his right shoe felt ready to fall off.

Chico kept running hard.

Suddenly the third baseman reached out to the left side of the bag to catch the throw.

"Hit the dirt!" yelled the coach.

Chico slid. He went to the right side of the bag, hooking it with his left foot. Safe!

The fans roared.

Chico called time. He laced his shoe tightly and tied a knot.

Boy! Chico thought. *If that shoe had come off, the fans sure would have had a laugh!*

Lead-off man Ray Ward smacked the first pitch right over the first baseman's head for a clean single. Chico scored, edging the Royals ahead, 3 to 2. Dale advanced to third.

Joe Ellis walked, filling the bases.

Time out was called, and the Braves' manager came out of the dugout. He walked to the mound and motioned in another pitcher.

The new man was a southpaw. He was short, stocky, and had a lot of speed. After a few warmup pitches, the game resumed. There were two outs.

Dutch Pierce stepped to the plate. With String Becker on deck, the Braves' new hurler was facing the Royals' strongest hitters. Dutch took a ball, then smashed a chest-high pitch over second base. Dale scored, followed by Ray Ward. Joe Ellis held up at third. The score was now 5 to 2.

That clout, and those scoring runs, did not make the Braves' southpaw look very happy. His infielders came in and talked with him.

When they returned to their positions, he walked up on the mound and faced the Royals' hardest hitter, String Becker.

He looked around the bases. There were men on first and third. You could tell he wished anybody else was at bat but String.

The little southpaw stepped on the rubber, made his stretch, and delivered.

String swung, and missed. "Strike one!"

The pitcher breezed in another. String started to swing, but didn't.

"Strike two!" said the umpire.

String stared at him but didn't say anything. Another pitch. String swung hard.

Swish!

"You're out!" shouted the umpire.

String stood at the plate a moment, staring at the pitcher. Then he tossed his bat aside, got his first-base mitt from the dugout, and trotted out to his position. Not a word left his lips.

"That's all right, String," said the coach. "You'll be up again."

Chico knew that was quite a blow for String. Imagine that little kid striking out String Becker!

Coach Day had Kenny Morton take Buddy's place at second and Louie Carlo take Joe Ellis's place in center field.

The Braves came up in the top of the fourth, anxious to do something about the score. A single and then a sacrifice bunt put a man in scoring position, but the Royals' defense was working fine. Not another man reached first.

The Royals hit hard at their turn at bat, but always into somebody's hands. Nothing serious happened until the sixth, when the Braves made a last desperate attempt to raise their score.

They managed to put across a run, making the score 5 to 3. Now, with two outs and two men on, they had their best chance of tying it up — or even going ahead of the Royals.

Their cleanup hitter was up. Already he had knocked out two doubles.

Anxiously, Don Drake looked toward the dugout at Coach Day.

"Pitch to him, Don," said the coach.

Chico backed up in left field. Louie Carlo stepped back, deeper in center. This batter was a long-ball hitter. If he met the ball squarely, it would go.

Chico waited.

C*rack!*

The sound of the bat connecting with the ball was like a shot. The white pill streaked out to deep left, curving toward the foul line.

"It's going over the fence!" someone in the bleachers yelled. "It's a homer!"

Chico raced back. Near the fence, he turned and looked over his shoulder. The ball was coming down a few feet inside fair territory. It was over his head.

He leapt high. *Smack!* The ball struck the pocket of his glove and stayed there.

Chico trotted in with the ball. His heart hammered with triumph. Ahead of him, his teammates were jumping with joy. Fans were cheering.

"Beautiful catch, Chico! Nice leap!"

"You saved the game for us, Chico!" Coach Day's eyes and face were bright as Chico approached. "Best catch I've seen in months!"

"Thank you, Coach," Chico said. And then he stood there while every member of the team shook his hand. String was last in line. He gripped Chico's hand lightly, then let go.

Chico was sure that String shook his hand only because the others did.

That night Buddy came to visit Chico. They went over the list of batting averages. String was leading with a whopping .397. Buddy's average was .388, Chico's .297.

"String is a much better hitter than either

of us," said Chico. "I wish I could hit as well as he does."

"Who doesn't?" said Buddy.

Chico thought about it awhile. "I'll try harder," he said finally. "Maybe if I hit better, String won't make fun of me so much. I know he doesn't like me."

"Oh, sure he does," said Buddy. "That's just his way, Chico. He's always ragging on people."

Chico shrugged. He remembered how lightly String had gripped his hand that afternoon. "Maybe," he said.

Nevertheless, he made up his mind to use a different bat. Maybe he couldn't beat String's average, but it wouldn't hurt to try.

On Monday the Royals played the Colts. When Chico batted, he gripped the long, yellow wood near the knob and swung at the pitches with all his might. The bat was an inch longer than the one he had used in previous games. It was the same size String and some of the bigger boys were using.

But the bat didn't help Chico. He struck out.

The next time he was up, he hit a dribbling grounder to the pitcher. He made a shoestring catch of a fly ball, though, which kept the Colts from scoring two runs. The Royals squeezed through with a win, 8 to 7.

Chico went without a hit.

The next game was a rematch against the Lions. Chico used the same long bat. He was sure he'd clout the ball today. Just one pitch — the right one — was all it would take to blast it over the fence.

But Chico didn't clout the ball. He hardly touched it. He went down swinging twice.

"C'mon, Chico!" yelled String. "Quit aiming for that fence! You'll never hit it then!"

Chico blushed.

On top of his poor showing at the plate, he also missed a high fly in the field that accounted for one of the Lions' runs. It was a bad day for Chico. Coach Day took him out in the fourth inning and put in Louie Carlo.

"You're trying too hard at the plate, Chico," said the coach. "You're too tense."

Chico, though, knew what his trouble was better than anyone.

The Lions blasted Frankie off the mound in the fifth inning. Don Drake held them to three hits, but the Lions were roaring. They took home the win, 9 to 3.

Perhaps, thought Chico, he had better not use the long yellow bat anymore. He would use the one he always batted with. Even though he'd never socked a homer with it, he had been able to get hits. And that's what counted most.

✿   ✿   ✿

On Monday they played the Marlins. After the game, the boys were going to a picnic at Orchard Falls Park.

The Marlins had a right-hander on the mound, Dick Mills, who could throw sharp curves and knucklers. Chico wasn't worried. He was confident he could hit anything the pitcher threw to him. He was going to use his old bat again.

"These guys are a cinch," String Becker said. The Royals were sitting in the dugout, watching the Marlins take their infield practice. "We trounced them twelve to one in the first round. We ought to be able to do it again."

"We'll make it a shutout this time," said Dutch Pierce.

Infield practice ended, and the game started. Dick Mills mowed Ray and Joe down with curves, but he couldn't fool

Dutch. Dutch blistered an inside pitch past the third baseman for a single. String acted anxious to send one over the fence, but four balls gave him a stroll to first.

This was a chance for the Royals to score. But with two strikes on him, Billy Hubble swung at a knuckler that must have looked as big as a balloon to him. Strike three, and the sides changed.

The Marlins' lead-off man punched out a single over short and then stole second. An error on shortstop Ray Ward put another man on. The man on second stayed there.

"C'mon! Look alive!" yelled String at first base. "Let's get 'em!"

Frankie worked hard on the third man, a left-hand hitter. A one-bouncer came back at him. Frankie caught it, spun, and whipped the ball to second. Ray stepped on the bag, then pegged to first.

A double play!

The cleanup hitter was a tall, husky right-hander. Chico moved back a dozen steps in left field. He remembered the first game with the Marlins. This guy had driven one to deep left. If it hadn't gone foul, it would have been a homer.

Crack! The ball whizzed out to left field like a torpedo. Chico stepped back a little and caught it easily. He knew that if he hadn't played deep for that hitter, he wouldn't have caught that ball.

"Nice catch, Chico," Coach Day said as Chico came running in. "Pick up a bat. You're up after Buddy."

Buddy singled.

Chico walked to the plate. He was using his regular bat now. He was sure he could hit whatever pitch Mills threw to him.

"Strike!" He had let that one go by.

Another pitch. A hook. Chico swung. Missed.

"Strike two!"

Chico stepped out of the box, and the umpire called time. Chico adjusted his belt, pulled his helmet down tighter, and stepped back into the box.

Mills threw two more pitches, both balls. Now the count was two and two.

The next pitch came in. A hook. Chico swung. *Whiff!*

"Strike three!" said the umpire.

Chico turned glumly, tossed his bat and helmet aside, and walked back to the dugout. He shook his head. He couldn't understand why he had missed those pitches. He just couldn't.

Dale Hunt flied out. Then Frankie started a rally with a hot single through short. The Royals scored twice before the Marlins got them out.

They managed to keep the Marlins scoreless for that inning.

Chico was up again in the third. String and Billy were on base. This was a chance for him to get some RBIs.

"Strike one!"

"Strike two!"

Chico couldn't believe it. Those hooks looked so easy to hit.

Then came the knuckler. The ball turned so slowly you could see the seams. Chico swung.

"You're out!" shouted the umpire.

Angrily, Chico tossed his bat aside as if it were the bat's fault that he hadn't got a hit. He trembled as he returned to the dugout. He was ashamed to face anyone.

"That's all right, Chico," Coach Day said comfortingly. "You're too anxious. You'll hit it."

In spite of Chico's failure to hit, the Royals picked up two more runs. Then the Marlins pushed across three runs at their turn at bat, making the score 4 to 3, Royals' favor.

The Royals scored twice again in the fourth, bringing their score to 6. Chico ended their at-bat by popping up. At least this time he'd gotten the feel of the ball.

Chico ran out to the field, wondering what he was doing wrong. He tore up a handful of grass, and flung it angrily behind him. Three times at bat and not one hit!

The Marlins began to hit and drove in a run. Then a man laid down a neat bunt toward third. Neither Frankie nor Dutch could get to it in time.

As Frankie released the first pitch to the next batter, the runner on first stole second. Dale didn't make the play on him. The man on third might try to run home.

The score was now 6 to 4. There were two men on and no outs.

Chico saw the next batter come to the plate, but he paid him little attention. He was thinking about his own hitting. It seemed impossible that he couldn't hit that big fat ball Mills threw. You would think he had never hit before!

Frankie stretched, then pitched. *Crack!*

Chico saw the ball shoot into the air toward left — *deep* left. His eyes widened, and just for an instant he glanced at the batter, who was now scrambling for first base.

It was the Marlins' slugger! Their long-ball hitter!

Chico turned and raced back as fast as his legs could carry him. He looked over his shoulder and saw the ball streak over his head! It hit the ground and bounced to the fence. Chico ran after it, picked it up, and pegged it in.

Dutch Pierce caught it and relayed it home. The runner was racing in. He slid, dust exploding in front of his feet. Dale put the ball on him.

"Safe!" yelled the plate umpire.

A home run!

Chico felt terrible. It was his fault. He had been thinking so much about his poor hitting, he had neglected to watch who was batting.

Kenny Morton took his place after that, but neither team scored again. The Marlins won, 7 to 6.

String Becker glared at Chico as they walked off the field.

"You lost the game for us, you know that?" he cried. "You knew that guy hits a long ball. Why didn't you back up when he came to bat?"

"I know. I'm sorry," said Chico.

"Sorry, yeah!" said String with disgust. "That helps a lot now!"

13

"All right, boys!" said Coach Day. "Don't forget the picnic at Orchard Falls Park!"

Chico headed straight toward the gate. His head was down. String's strong words were still ringing in his ears.

"Chico!" called the coach. "You're coming to the picnic, aren't you?"

Chico turned and paused. Yes, he wanted to go. But if everyone blamed him for losing the game, why should he? How could he enjoy himself?

"Come on, Chico!" said Buddy. "We'll hike and swim and have a lot of fun."

"Sure!" said Coach Day, smiling. "Don't worry about today. It's all over with. Get home, change your clothes, and I'll pick you up in fifteen or twenty minutes."

Chico thought about it a moment. "Okay," he said, "I'll be ready."

Orchard Falls Park was ten miles beyond the city limits. A huge playground area was on the right side as you drove in from the highway. Farther in was the large lake. Sitting atop a high platform, a sun helmet on his head, was the lifeguard. He was busy watching the swimmers.

At the far edge of the lake were the high, frosty-white falls. A heavy mist hovered near the bottom, where the water dropped into the lake with a loud, steady roar.

Scattered in dozens of places under the trees were picnic tables and fireplaces. Three cars, including Coach Day's station wagon, hauled in the boys. They found two empty tables close to each other and put them end to end. Then the men began to prepare the dinner.

Most of the boys dashed to the bathhouse, where they changed into their bathing suits.

"I don't really want to go swimming yet," said String to Buddy. "Let's go on a hike along the gorge."

"Okay!" said Buddy. "Want to come along, Chico?"

"Does he have to go everyplace you go?" String snorted.

Buddy smiled. "No. But he's never been here. Have you, Chico?"

Chico shot an icy look at String. String was always making fun of him. "That's all right, Buddy. You two go alone."

"Never mind. Come on," said String. "I'm only kidding."

Only kidding. He always says that, thought Chico. *But I know he means it.*

"I just hope we don't come across any snakes," said String. "I hate them!"

"Yikes — me, too!" said Buddy, laughing.

They told Coach Day where they were going, then started toward the woods. Near the foot of the falls, they found the path that led up the steep, tree-filled hillside.

"My dad told me the park people cleared out a deep swimming hole up here," Buddy commented. "They thought the park could have two swimming areas. But most people stay down at the lower one because of the falls."

They paused awhile and watched the water gush over the falls. The thunderous roar made it hard to hear anything else.

They went on, climbing higher and higher. String and Buddy walked side by side, with Chico trailing behind them. On both sides of the path were smelly dead leaves, pine cones, and broken twigs.

Chico felt excitement bubbling inside him. There was adventure here, and danger. Danger because the steep path was slippery from the rain that had poured the day before — and only inches to their left was the sharp drop of the gorge.

Soon they came to the upper pond. They stopped and threw rocks in for a while.

Then Buddy said, "Let's keep going, up to the overlook, okay?"

"Shouldn't we be heading back?" asked Chico.

String turned. His eyes mocked Chico. "What's the matter? Scared to go any higher?"

"No. But maybe dinner's ready. By the time we get back —"

"Don't worry," said String. "There's plenty of food for everybody."

Chico shrugged. He was sorry he had said anything.

They continued slowly up the path, looking at the water below them and the lake birds flying around in slow, lazy circles.

Suddenly something on the ground caught Chico's eyes. It was at the edge of the path — a snake about three feet long!

"Look out!" he yelled. "Snake!"

Just as he yelled, it slithered across the path behind the two boys. Buddy spun, his eyes wide. String spun around, too. His face turned white. He saw the snake and jumped back.

One foot slid onto some leaves at the edge of the path, and he lost his balance. He fell, then slid on his back down the steep bank. He tried to stop himself but couldn't. "Help! I — I can't swim!" he screamed.

The next instant he was falling through space, his feet sprawled out in front of him. Far below, he struck the water and disappeared.

He sank!" cried Buddy. "I can't see him!" Panic was in his face and eyes.

Frozen with shock and horror, Chico was unable to move.

"What are we going to do?" Buddy moaned. "He'll probably drown!"

Suddenly Chico came to life. He quickly started stripping off his T-shirt. "I'll dive in after him," he said.

"Dive in? Are you crazy? That's about thirty feet! You could hurt yourself bad!"

"I won't get hurt," Chico assured him.

"You said yourself there was a deep pool cleared out down below here!"

Buddy stared down at the water. "Look!" He pointed. "There's String! He came up! But he looks . . . he looks unconscious or something."

Chico pulled off his sneakers and socks. Carefully he hurried down the bank a few feet, stood in diving position for a moment, then pushed himself forward. He dived gracefully, his feet together behind him, his hands stretched over his head and spread slightly apart. It seemed a long time that he was suspended there in the air, holding his breath. Then he struck the smooth, mirror-like top of the water. He went down deep, then swam back up to the surface.

The water was cool, and he shivered. He gulped in fresh air, whipped his hair away from his face, and looked around for String.

About twenty feet away from him — in

the direction of the falls — he saw String bobbing in the water.

"String!" Chico yelled. "String!"

String didn't move. Terror took hold of Chico. Maybe Buddy was right. String was probably unconscious!

Chico started swimming as swiftly as he could toward String. The falls were not too far away. If he didn't get to String soon . . .

The horrible thought of what would happen made Chico swim even faster. Suddenly he didn't see String. String had gone down!

No! There he was again!

Chico swam harder than he had ever swum in his life. The gap between them began to close. At long last he reached String, put his left hand under String's chin, then turned and swam toward the shore.

The current was strong against them, but Chico swam with powerful strokes. He reached the shore, pulled up String beside him with panting breath, and held String's head in his arms.

String's eyes were closed. Suddenly he coughed hard, sputtering water.

"String!" Chico cried. "String! Can you talk?"

"Who — who is it?" gasped String.

The words were like music to Chico. His eyes brightened. "It's me! Chico!"

"Where — where's Buddy?"

"Up on the path. I'll bet he went after Coach Day."

String didn't say any more. Chico looked at his wet face. It was pale and tired-looking. Chico grew worried. Would String be all right?

After what seemed like a long while, he heard voices nearby. Then Coach Day and the other men came hurrying along the narrow shore. They saw him and String and rushed forward.

"How is he, Chico?"

"He was talking to me," said Chico.

"Good! Here, let me have him." Coach Day put his arms around String's shoulders. "String! Are you all right?"

String turned his head. His eyes opened. "I guess I swallowed a lot of water, Coach. My stomach feels full."

Coach Day smiled. "We'd better get you to a doctor, String. From what Buddy told us, that was quite a long fall."

"Chico saved my life, Coach," said String. "He dived in after me. That took a lot of nerve, Coach. You know it?"

The doctor could find nothing seriously wrong with String, except that he suffered slightly from shock. However, he advised that String be sent to a hospital.

String stayed in the hospital only a day. He was told, though, that he should rest for a week. During that time the Royals played two games. They squeezed a win over the Bombers, 8 to 7. Then they started off round three with a loss to the Braves, 5 to 2.

Chico got a hit in each game. He felt he was getting back in stride.

On August 3, the Royals played the Colts. With String back on first base, the Royals were their old selves again. But no, thought Chico. Something was different from before.

The Colts pounded Frankie's pitches, but a Royals man was always there to catch the ball. Their defense was like a brick wall.

The fans gave String a rousing cheer when he stepped to the plate. There were two men on. It was a good chance to score.

String took two strikes, then went down swinging. Ground balls to short and first ended the Royals' threat. The Colts were playing well defensively, too.

The innings went on without a score. The game turned into a pitchers' duel. Several men from both teams got on bases, but tight playing kept them from scoring.

In the fifth, the Colts started to build

some momentum. The first batter singled, then stole second. Then Frankie threw a hook that went wild. The runner raced to third.

"Let's settle down!" yelled Coach Day.

String and Dutch Pierce walked to the mound to talk with Frankie. They returned to their positions and started a steady flow of infield chatter.

Out in left field, Chico watched the batter closely. Here was a strong hitter, he remembered. He didn't hit the ball very high, but low and hard.

Crack! A smashing hit to left. It sailed over third baseman Dutch Pierce's head in a long clothesline drive.

Chico moved back. The ball was coming like a bullet. It was going over his head!

He leapt. *Plop!* He had it!

The runner on third tagged up and made

a beeline for home. The way the game was going, that run could mean plenty. It could win the ball game.

Chico reared back and pegged the ball in as hard as he could. It went over Dutch's head and bounced once. Then Dale caught it at the plate and tagged the runner.

"You're out!" yelled the umpire.

The Royals fans stomped on the bleachers and screamed.

"Beautiful peg, Chico!" Dutch called.

"Thataway, Chico!" String shouted from first. "Great arm!"

Chico glowed with pride.

The next man grounded out, and the inning was over.

With one out and no men on, String came to the plate. This time he cut hard at the first pitch and struck it solidly. Even as the ball sailed far and high, everybody knew just where it was going.

Over the fence! A home run!

The Colts' momentum was gone, and their final at-bat was scoreless. The game ended, 1 to 0.

The whole Royals team crowded around String and Frankie. They happily pounded their backs and shook their hands. String's smile stretched from ear to ear.

Then he saw Chico. He came forward and put an arm around Chico's shoulders.

"Boy, Chico!" he said. "You really threw that apple! It was perfect!"

"Thanks," said Chico, smiling. "You really *hit* that apple!"

"Thanks, Chico. Look, after you change clothes and eat, come over to my house, will you? I have something I want to ask you."

Chico nodded. "Okay!"

He knew now what was different from before. It was String.

✿   ✿   ✿

At home Chico took off his uniform, washed, put on clean clothes, and ate. All the while he wondered why String wanted him to go to his house.

It was almost twilight when he left. He met Buddy on the way, and Buddy went with him. Chico didn't think String would mind.

"Hi, Chico. Hi, Buddy," said String as he opened the door for them. "Come on in."

The boys sat in the living room. String left the room for a minute. When he returned, he was wearing a brand-new bathing suit. He grinned sheepishly.

"I don't have anything to give you to thank you for saving my life, Chico," he said plainly. "In fact, I'm going to ask you for something." He took a deep breath and blurted out, "Will you teach me how to swim?"

Chico gazed at him solemnly. "Okay, but I want something in return."

String and Buddy looked at him with surprise. "You do?" String said.

"Yes," Chico replied. He broke out in a big smile. "I want you to teach me how to hit with that long yellow bat! Next season, I want to put one over the fence like you do!"

String and Buddy laughed out loud. "It's a deal!" String said. "I'll meet you at the ballpark first thing tomorrow morning. But now you guys scram. I feel like an idiot standing around here in my bathing suit!"

Still laughing, Buddy and Chico headed for home.

Things are working out just fine, thought Chico happily. *Just fine.*

★ ★

★

READ ALL THE BOOKS

In The

New MATT CHRISTOPHER Sports Library!

BASEBALL FLYHAWK
978-1-59953-354-4

THE BASKET COUNTS
978-1-59953-212-7

CATCH THAT PASS
978-1-59953-105-2

CENTER COURT STING
978-1-59953-106-9

THE COMEBACK CHALLENGE
978-1-59953-211-0

DIRT BIKE RACER
978-1-59953-113-7

DIRT BIKE RUNAWAY
978-1-59953-215-8

THE GREAT QUARTERBACK SWITCH
978-1-59953-216-5

THE HOCKEY MACHINE
978-1-59953-214-1

ICE MAGIC
978-1-59953-112-0

THE KID WHO ONLY HIT HOMERS
978-1-59953-107-6

LACROSSE FACE-OFF
978-1-59953-355-1

LONG-ARM QUARTERBACK
978-1-59953-114-4

MOUNTAIN BIKE MANIA
978-1-59953-108-3

POWER PITCHER
978-1-59953-356-8

RETURN OF THE HOME RUN KID
978-1-59953-213-4

SHOOT FOR THE HOOP
978-1-59953-357-5

SKATEBOARD TOUGH
978-1-59953-115-1

SNOWBOARD MAVERICK
978-1-59953-116-8

SNOWBOARD SHOWDOWN
978-1-59953-109-0

SOCCER HALFBACK
978-1-59953-110-6

SOCCER SCOOP
978-1-59953-117-5

THE TEAM THAT COULDN'T LOSE
978-1-59953-358-2

TOUGH TO TACKLE
978-1-59953-359-9

★ ★